# BiLL & Ted's EXCELLENT adventure™

# THE GUIDE TO A RODACIOUS LIFE

by Steve Behling
Illustrated by Chris Piascik

Little, Brown and Company
New York Boston

Little, Brown and Company
Hachette Book Group
1290 Avenue of the Americas, New York, NY 10104
Visit us at LBYR.com

First Edition: July 2020

Little, Brown and Company is a division of Hachette Book Group, Inc.
The Little, Brown name and logo are trademarks of Hachette Book Group, Inc.

The publisher is not responsible for websites (or their content)
that are not owned by the publisher.

Library of Congress Control Number 2019955226

ISBNs: 978-0-316-53845-9 (paper over board), 978-0-316-53844-2 (ebook),
978-0-316-53848-0 (ebook), 978-0-316-53843-5 (ebook)

Printed in the United States of America

WOR

10 9 8 7 6 5 4 3 2 1

# Greetings, My Excellent Friends!

You now hold in your hands a book from the future! Except you're reading it in the present. Which is really the past for the people who wrote this book in the future!

Makes sense, right?

No?

Don't worry, you'll get the hang of it—just like Bill S. Preston, Esquire, and Ted "Theodore" Logan did. In fact, they helped put together this book of most outstanding tips, tricks, and life hacks to help you navigate life's excellent adventures and bogus journeys.

So, turn the page, and enter a most bodacious world of peace and musical harmony.
Be excellent to each other,

*Rufus*

# How to Have a Most Excellent Adventure

Anyone can have an adventure! That's why they call them "adventures!" Actually, that's probably not why. We have no idea. But adventures are totally cool! And you should have one! Or maybe even three! Here are some helpful hints to make your own adventure. Excellent!

## HINT!

Surround yourself with totally awesome people. You probably have a whole bunch around you already. But if not, just use your time machine and round up some from history!

## HINT!

When in doubt, play air guitar. It is most highly recommended and can be used to highlight favorite moments of your excellent adventure.

(FOR EXAMPLE, NOW WOULD BE A GOOD TIME TO PLAY AIR GUITAR.)

## HINT!

Be excellent to each other. No matter where you go or who you meet, you must do this. Do not be heinous. Because that *would* be heinous. And then the Circuits of Time might collapse on themselves or something.

MOST EXCELLENT

# How to Speak Like Bill and Ted

| WORD | MEANING |
| --- | --- |
| Bogus | Uncool |
| Bodacious | Cool |
| Dude | A fellow person |
| Egregious | Extraordinary, in a bad way |
| Excellent | Extraordinary |
| Heinous | Disgusting |
| Most | To the greatest extent |
| No way | Expression of amazement |
| Outstanding | Marked by excellence |
| Totally | Wholly and completely |
| Triumphant | Magnificent, splendid |
| Yes way | Response to "No way" |

If you wish to sound like the most bodacious Bill S. Preston, Esquire, and Ted "Theodore" Logan, then you must know these words. Not only must you know them, but you must say them to your friends every day. Failure to do so will earn you a one-way ticket to Oates Military, which we don't need to tell you is TOTALLY HEINOUS.

## EXAMPLE

"The math test was bogus."

"Our band is most bodacious."

"How's it goin', dude?"

"We have flunked—most egregiously."

"Be excellent to each other."

"Napoleon's manners are most heinous."

"That is most excellent!"

"No way!"

"That song is most outstanding."

"That is totally awesome."

"We need a triumphant video!"

"Yes way!"

"I'M BILL S. PRESTON, ESQUIRE!"

"AND I'M TED `THEODORE` LOGAN!"

"and we're WYLD STALLYNS!"

— BILL S. PRESTON, ESQUIRE, AND TED "THEODORE" LOGAN

# Philosophy Dos and Don'ts by So-crates

Good advice is good advice, no matter whether it comes from the present, the future...or the past! In this case, from 410 BC, a time when much of the world looked like the cover of one of the most excellent albums of all time. Our extremely helpful Dos and Don'ts come courtesy of the father of modern thought and the teacher of Plato: the most bodacious philosophizer, So-crates!

  **DO** REMEMBER THAT TRUE WISDOM CONSISTS OF KNOWING THAT YOU KNOW NOTHING.

 **DON'T** SPEAK TO STRANGERS AT THE MALL—IT IS RUDE, AND THEY WILL MOCK YOU.

  **DO** GO WITH THE FLOW, AND ENJOY STRANGE, NEW EXPERIENCES.

 **DON'T** PRETEND THAT OUR LIVES ARE MORE THAN SPECKS OF DUST FALLING THROUGH THE FINGERS OF TIME.

 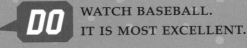 **DO** WATCH BASEBALL. IT IS MOST EXCELLENT.

# Create Your Own
# Band Name, Dude!

If you want to be truly awesome, you must make your own bodacious band! But you're saying, "Book, I can't play an instrument. I can't sing. Also, I do not own a private jet in which I could fly from concert to concert." You'll be glad to know that *none of that matters*! All that matters is choosing a band name. Choose one word from Column A, and one from Column B to make your own!

| Column A | Column B |
|---|---|
| Awesome | Lizzerds |
| Bodacious | Panthrrrs |
| Egregious | Lionz |
| Impressive | Möngoose* |
| Majestic | Yetis |
| Most Excellent | Platypüs |
| Non-henious | Groundhawgs |
| Vicious | Skwidz |
| Wyld | Stallyns |

*(Möngeese? We're not sure what a bunch of them are called.)

# Napoleon's Favorite Snacks

Have you ever heard the phrase "Enjoy snacks like an 18th-century French general and/or emperor"? No? That's because we totally made it up. Still! We think it's true, and the person best suited to give you a list of most bodacious snackage is Napoleon himself.

*La glace!* Ice cream!

*La glace!* Ice cream!

*Mon empire pour la glace!* My empire for ice cream!

*Vive la glace!!!!* Long live ice cream!!!!

# Five Things You Should Know About Time Travel

Now that we think about it, there are probably more than five things you should know about time travel. But according to our most excellent friend from the future, Rufus, you just need to worry about the ones below. And if none of this makes sense, don't worry. Rufus is a professional.

## THING #1

When getting out of the time machine and meeting new people, it's important to say, "Greetings, my excellent friends."

GREETINGS, MY EXCELLENT friends

## THING #2

The first time you're traveling along the Circuits of Time, it can be a little freaky. Bring a pair of sunglasses. That'll help.

# THING #3

Always carry pudding cups and chewing gum. You never know when you might get stranded in 1,000,000 BC and need something to eat (or use to fix the antenna on top of your phone booth).

# THING #4

When in doubt, consult the *Circuits of Time Directory* book that comes with your time machine. It has the coordinates of any possible time you'd like to visit. Except Monday. Nobody wants to go to Monday.

# THING #5

If you travel to the Austrian Empire in 1805, be careful that Napoleon doesn't try to blow you up. He's kind of a jerk like that.

# What to Do If Your Dad Threatens to Send You to Oates Military Academy

Like the old saying goes, "There comes a time in every person's life when their dad threatens to send them to Oates Military Academy." This is something that's commonly said and everyone knows, which is why we're talking about it. Anyway. If, for some terrible reason, *your* father threatens you with such heinous punishment, we recommend following these five simple steps.

**STEP ONE**

Do not fail history class. If you fail history class, your dad will most surely give you a one-way ticket to Oates Military Academy.

**STEP TWO**

Get a time machine and round up some totally famous historical figures, then bring them back to your time to deliver a most incredible history report.

**STEP THREE**

If you do not have access to a time machine or totally famous historical figures, then you should study hard and do really well in class.

**STEP FOUR**

And if your dad tells you that he spoke to Colonel Oates this morning and that the colonel is most anxious to meet you, *believe him*, and repeat Steps Two or Three as needed.

**STEP FIVE**

Pass history class.

# Be EXCELLENT TO EACH OTHER.

→ BILL S. PRESTON, ESQUIRE

# Abraham Lincoln's Party
# Dos and Don'ts

Having a most triumphant party will make anyone's day. So we asked one of the greatest presidents in American history, Abraham Lincoln, to provide some tips to make your next party the most bodacious one yet.

 **DO** INVITE ANYWHERE BETWEEN ONE SCORE AND FOURSCORE GUESTS, GIVE OR TAKE SEVEN PEOPLE.

 **DON'T** INVITE JOHN WILKES BOOTH. NO ONE BRINGS A PARTY DOWN LIKE JOHN WILKES BOOTH.

 **DO** SERVE PUDDING CUPS! EVERYONE LOVES PUDDING CUPS!

 **DON'T** EAT ALL THE PUDDING CUPS YOURSELF. THIS IS RUDE AND WILL LEAD TO AN AWFUL STOMACHACHE. THERE ARE NO GOOD REMEDIES FOR THAT SORT OF THING IN 1864.

 **DO** PARTY ON, DUDES!

# How to Make Friends with Difficult Dudes

Whether you're traveling the Circuits of Time to visit Genghis Khan or just sitting in Mr. Ryan's history class, you're going to meet a lot of different people. Some of those people will be totally friendly. Some will be most non-friendly. Luckily, we have a few tips to help you navigate those potentially heinous waters.

## TIP #1

Be excellent to everyone. Treat your history teacher with the same respect as you would the number one guitarist of all time.

## TIP #2

If someone says they're going to put you in an iron maiden, this may sound totally cool. It is not. So do whatever you can to avoid someone saying that.

## TIP #3

Don't insult anyone's manners, no matter how heinous they are. Genghis Khan eating like, well, Genghis Khan is no reason to make him feel bad.

# What to Do If There are Strange Things Afoot at the Convenience Store

Have you ever been to the convenience store when dark clouds show up in the sky, and a phone booth appears in a flash of bright, blue light? No? Then we must not go to the same place. Anyway, when something strange happens while you're out getting a late-night snack, you'll want to know what to do.

# What to Do If You Have a Crush on a Totally Excellent Person

Did you know that you might meet a totally excellent person when you're traveling through time? And that you might get a crush on them? You didn't? Well, now you do! And we have some simple steps you can follow to make the most of the moment.

**TIP #1** First say, "I bring to you a message of love."

**TIP #2** Then recite some song lyrics.

**TIP #3** Ask your crush to the prom.

**NOTE** This works with most songs, but not "Row, Row, Row Your Boat," which is a totally non-romantic song.

18

# How to Find the Most Triumphant

When you are hungry and not near a convenience store, what do you do? Starve? No, you go to the food court at the mall! But how will you decide what to eat? Use this flowchart to make your most excellent choice.

# What to Do If Your Future Self Suddenly Appears and Says a Bunch of Stuff You Totally Don't Understand

Has this ever happened to you? You're just standing there outside the convenience store, and suddenly, you appear right in front of you! Only it's not you. We mean, it *is* you. But it's you from the future. Future You. What should you say? What should you do? We have some suggestions.

## TIP #1

Listen! Open your ears and hear what Future You has to say. They'll probably have all sorts of totally useful info that will affect you in the future.

## TIP #2
Trust! Most of the stuff Future You says won't make any sense. Like, if Future You says, "Don't forget to wind your watch!" you're gonna think, *Why should I do that, Future Me? Also, I don't have a watch!* But just trust Future You.

## TIP #3
Get a watch.

## TIP #4
And wind it.

## TIP #5
Play air guitar! End every encounter with Future You with a totally awesome air guitar solo. Future You will be glad you did, and so will You You!

# How to Fix a Totally **BroKen** Time-Machine Antenna

Do you want to know what is most un-righteous about traveling throug the Circuits of Time? No? We don't blame you. But you need to be prepared for any bumps in the road of time travel. So here's what to do in the event the antenna on your time machine breaks.

## YOU WILL NEED:
- MANY PUDDING CUPS (METAL*)
- A MOST PRODIGIOUS AMOUNT OF GUM
- GROUP OF BETWEEN 7-10 PEOPLE (INCLUDING HISTORICAL FRIENDS)

**STEP ONE:** AS A GROUP, OPEN PUDDING CUPS; EAT ALL THE PUDDING BECAUSE IT IS MOST WASTEFUL TO THROW OUT GOOD PUDDING.

**STEP TWO:** MAKE A NEW ANTENNA OUT OF THE EMPTY CUPS.

**STEP THREE:** CHEW THE GUM.

**STEP FOUR:** ALL THE GUM.

**STEP FIVE:** DO NOT SWALLOW THE GUM.

**STEP SIX:** WHEN GUM IS TOTALLY CHEWED, SPIT GUM INTO YOUR HAND. HAVE EVERYONE ELSE SPIT THEIR GUM INTO YOUR HAND.

**STEP SEVEN:** MAKE LARGE, GROSS, STICKY GUM WAD.

**STEP EIGHT:** PLACE NEW ANTENNA ON TOP OF TIME MACHINE WITH LARGE, GROSS, STICKY GUM WAD.

**STEP NINE:** RESUME YOUR TRIP THROUGH TIME!

"THIS HAS BEEN A MOST Excellent adventure."

↳TED "THEODORE" LOGAN

# What to Do If You're Having a
# Bogus Journey

**If you live long enough, you'll come to learn that not *all* journeys are excellent. Some of them are totally bogus. To help you in your hour of need, we've compiled a checklist of things you can do in the event you have a most bogus journey.**

☐ DON'T have a bogus journey. This seems totally obvious. But sometimes you just can't avoid having one, because life has a way of giving you a melvin✝ when you least expect it.

☐ Even in the face of most terrible times, continue to be excellent to each other. After all, you're all you've got.

☐ If, during the course of your bogus journey, you end up in Hell, don't be upset that it doesn't look like it did on all those metal album covers.

☐ Play some air guitar. While it won't get you out of your bogus journey, it will make you totally feel better for a few seconds.

☐ If you cross paths with an evil robot version of yourself during your bogus journey and they ask you to go for a ride in a van, **DO NOT** do this. That is a most egregiously awful idea.

+melvin [mel•vin; *noun*]: A frontal wedgie; it is most heinous.

# Here's a Totally Awesome Marriage Proposal YOU Can Use

We already talked about what to do if you have a crush on a totally excellent person. But what if you love them so much that you want to *marry* them? Instead of standing there all tongue-tied, you could use this marriage proposal. Just fill in the blanks, dude!

_____, as I
[name of person to whom you're totally proposing]

wander through this dark and lonely forest

of life, surrounded by various beasts...

bears, _____, squirrels,
[type of snake, plural]

not to mention small tree-growing lichen,

woodpeckers, slugs, _____,
[type of animal, plural]

Gila monsters. Oh no—that's the desert.

The point is, I promise you a most

_____ life.
[excellent / resplendent / other adjective]

What I'm trying to say is, will you marry me?

# How to **Not** be Excellent!

There are probably lots of reasons why you might not want to be excellent. Unfortunately, we couldn't think of one. So we had to travel to the year 2691 and ask Chuck De Nomolos for his foolproof plan on how to *not* be excellent.

# How to Not Be Excellent!
## By the Greatest Man in History,
# Chuck De Nomolos

- ## Do not do excellent things!

This is surprisingly easy, especially if you are as unpleasant a fellow as myself.

- ## Use sinister robot duplicates to enforce your will!

Ask your parents for help before making the sinister robot duplicates. I do not wish to be liable for any mishap.

- ## Destroy the insipid band Wyld Stallyns!

Before those fools can deliver their musical message of peace to millions, squash them like bugs—thus ensuring the future rule of me, De Nomolos!

# What to Do If You're Replaced by an Evil Robot from the Future

What are the odds of us mentioning evil robot duplicates on page 31, only for you to turn the page and find out what to do if you're replaced by an evil robot from the future on pages 32 and 33? As it turns out, they're most outstanding! So follow these five simple rules, and you'll live to make music that will totally shape the future.

## RULE 1
Stay totally cool.

## RULE 2
Make a Good Robot You to fight the Evil Robot You.

## RULE 3
Ask your parents for help before making the Good Robot You. We don't want to be liable for any mishap, which would be most unfortunate.

## RULE 4
Watch the Good Robot You defeat the Evil Robot You!

## RULE 5
Play victorious air guitar!

# Games You Can Play with the Grim Reaper

Let's say you meet Death. You might say, "How's it hangin', Death?" And Death, aka the Grim Reaper, is going to say something totally sad and depressing. And then he might make you go home with him. But not if you challenge him to a game, and win! Then he totally has to take you home! Here's a short list of games you could try.

CHARADES

DING-DONG DITCH*

DODGEBALL

GO FISH

HANGMAN

HIDE-AND-SEEK

HOPSCOTCH

MOTHER, MAY I?

POKER

RED LIGHT,
GREEN LIGHT

TAG

TETHERBALL

TIC-TAC-TOE

*Technically not a game, but still fun

35

# How to Succeed at Practically Anything

Who doesn't like to succeed at practically anything? Even De Nomolos wants to succeed, except he wants to succeed at being evil, which is most non-triumphant. Our point is, everyone could use a little help to be their most outstanding. So we asked Station for their expert guide at how to succeed.

**STEP ONE**

STATION!

**STEP TWO**

STATION!!

**STEP THREE**

STATION!!!

"YOU MAY BE A KING OR A LITTLE STREET SWEEPER, BUT SOONER OR LATER, you DANCE WITH the REAPER!

↳ THE GRIM REAPER

# INDEX